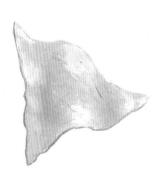
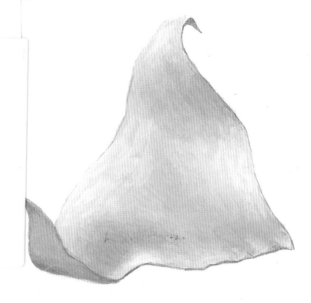

TOY BOAT

Randall de Sève • Loren Long

Philomel Books

A little boy had a toy boat.
He made it from a can, a cork, a yellow pencil, and some white cloth.

The boy loved the boat, and they were never apart.

They bathed together.

They slept together.

And every day, they would go down to the lake and sail all afternoon.

The boy held the boat by a string and never let go.

Most of the time, this was nice for the boat. But sometimes the little toy boat would look out at big boats gliding across the lake and wonder what it would feel like to sail free.

One blustery afternoon, a dark cloud rolled over the lake. The boy's mom pulled him back toward the house. Her tug made him drop the boat's string.

The boy cried out as the little toy boat floated away. "Boat!" he called. "Boat!" But nothing could be done.

Wind and rain pushed the little toy boat
into deep water. There it bobbed on high waves
topped with foam.

In time, a black and green tugboat with a row of old tires on its side chugged past. Its windows looked like tired eyes that seemed to say "Move along!" as it pushed the little toy boat aside with its wake.

The little toy boat worked so hard to stay afloat, it almost didn't see the giant ferry in its path. The ferry had two flags and a red smokestack, and a horn that bellowed, "Move along!"

A gust of wind blew the little toy boat out of the way just in time.

A speedboat raced by. Flat and sharp with flames on its side, its motor screamed, "Move along!" Its draft made the little boat's sail quiver.

Feeling small and scared, the little toy
boat drifted out toward a fleet of sailboats
racing home to get out of the rain.

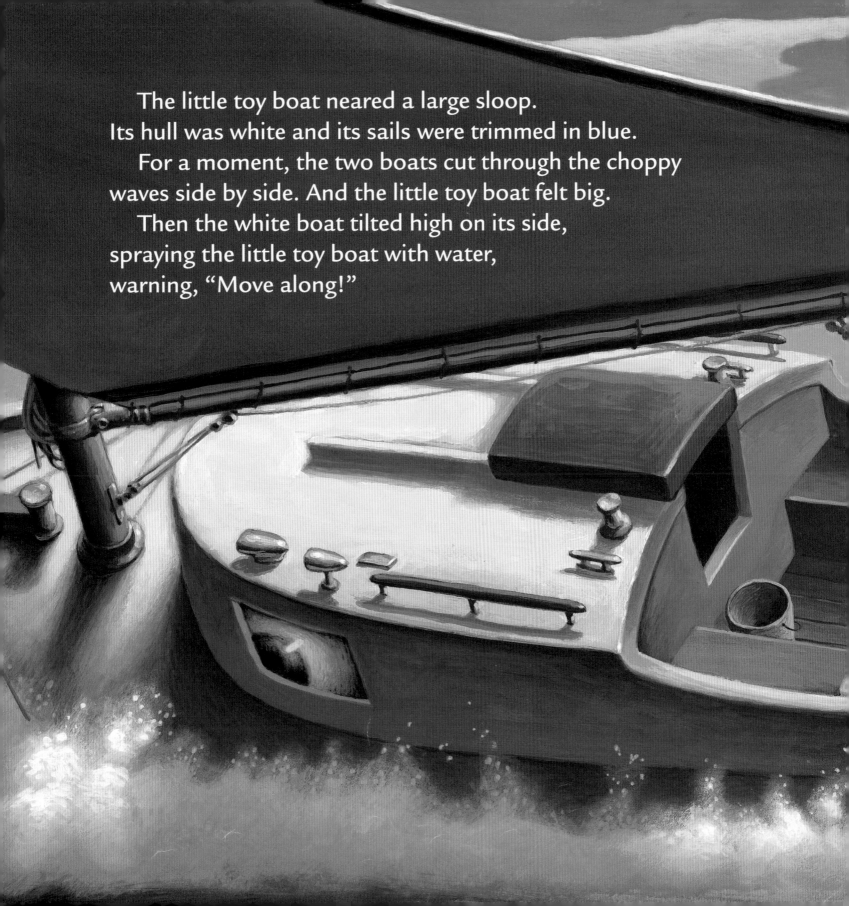

The little toy boat neared a large sloop.
Its hull was white and its sails were trimmed in blue.
For a moment, the two boats cut through the choppy
waves side by side. And the little toy boat felt big.
Then the white boat tilted high on its side,
spraying the little toy boat with water,
warning, "Move along!"

Its hull near full, its sail soaked, the little toy
boat looked like it would sink.
How it missed the boy!

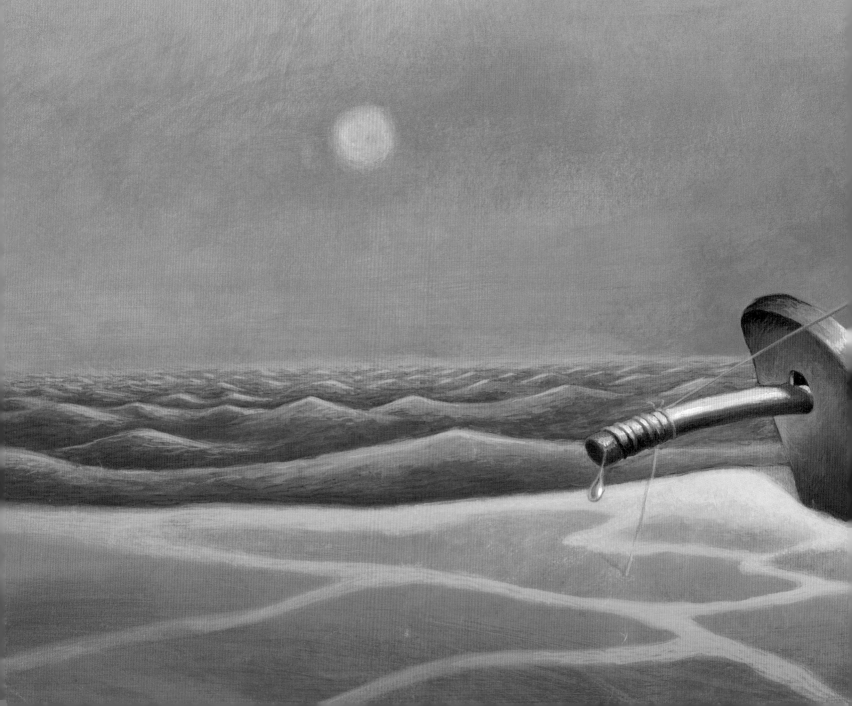

Under the yellow moon, the little toy boat
drifted all night, alone and scared.

But then, early in the morning—
"Put-put. Put-put."
   It was a humble little fishing boat way
out in the middle of the lake. Its paint was
peeling and the dents on its side said it knew
how it felt to be pushed around on the lake.
   The fishing boat spied the little toy boat
and carefully began to circle it. As it did,
something wonderful happened.

The little toy boat began to turn as well, and its sail caught a breeze. Soon it was sailing, really sailing, alongside the fishing boat. And the little toy boat felt strong! "I am moving along," it shouted to the wind.

It felt so good that it didn't notice when the fishing
boat motored on. It didn't notice the stone beach or
the yellow bench on the nearby shore.

And it didn't notice the boy.

Not until he called out, "Boat! Boat!"

The little toy boat waved its sail excitedly.

The boy waved back.

That night, they bathed together.

They slept together.

And the next day, they went down to the lake together. The boy held the boat by a string and every so often let go. But the little toy boat always came back. It knew just where it wanted to be.

For Paulina and Fia, with love   —RdS

For Tracy, Griffith and Graham   —LL

PATRICIA LEE GAUCH, EDITOR

PHILOMEL BOOKS
A division of Penguin Young Readers Group.
Published by The Penguin Group.
Penguin Group (USA) Inc., 375 Hudson Street, New York, NY 10014, U.S.A.
Penguin Group (Canada), 90 Eglinton Avenue East, Suite 700, Toronto, Ontario, Canada M4P 2Y3
(a division of Pearson Penguin Canada Inc.).
Penguin Books Ltd, 80 Strand, London WC2R 0RL, England.
Penguin Ireland, 25 St. Stephen's Green, Dublin 2, Ireland (a division of Penguin Books Ltd.).
Penguin Group (Australia), 250 Camberwell Road, Camberwell, Victoria 3124, Australia (a division of
Pearson Australia Group Pty Ltd).
Penguin Books India Pvt Ltd, 11 Community Centre, Panchsheel Park, New Delhi - 110 017, India.
Penguin Group (NZ), 67 Apollo Drive, Mairangi Bay, Auckland 1311, New Zealand (a division of Pearson
New Zealand Ltd.)
Penguin Books (South Africa) (Pty) Ltd, 24 Sturdee Avenue, Rosebank, Johannesburg 2196, South Africa.
Penguin Books Ltd, Registered Offices: 80 Strand, London WC2R 0RL, England.

Published simultaneously in Canada.   Manufactured in China by South China Printing Co. Ltd.
Design by Semadar Megged.   Text set in 19-point Legacy Sans Medium.
The illustrations are rendered in acrylic.

Library of Congress Cataloging-in-Publication Data
De Sève, Randall.   Toy boat / Randall de Sève ; illustrated by Loren Long.   p. cm.
Summary: A toy boat gets separated from his owner and has an adventure on the high seas.
[1. Toys—Fiction. 2. Boats and boating—Fiction.] I. Long, Loren, ill. II. Title.
PZ7.D4504Toy 2007   [E]—dc22   2006026281

ISBN 978-0-399-24374-5
1 3 5 7 9 10 8 6 4 2
First Impression